Light Musings

A Poetic Narrative

By:

Xtina Marie

A HellBound Books Publishing LLC Book
Houston TX

**A HellBound Books LLC
Publication**

Copyright © 2018 by HellBound Books Publishing LLC
All Rights Reserved
Cover and art design Jason McIntyre

No part of this book may be reproduced, stored in a retrieval system,
or transmitted by any means, electronic, mechanical, photocopying,
recording or otherwise without written permission from the author
This book is a work of fiction. Names, characters, places and
incidents are entirely fictitious or are used fictitiously and any
resemblance to actual persons, living or dead, events or locales is
purely coincidental.

www.hellboundbookspublishing.com

Contents

Micro Shorts:

Long Distance
High on Love
8:29 Forever
Everything and Nothing
Broke Down on a Country Road
Exhilarating
He Doesn't Say It Back
Christmas with You
What He Gave Her
Conspiracy Theories & Aliens

About the Author

Xtina Marie

Acknowledgements

A special thank you to E.A. Barker for writing me a fantastic blurb. Again.

Thank you to Jason McIntyre for Light Musing's beautiful cover, and for being patient with me when I had *no idea* what I wanted.

Dedications

To: Jenny, you will always be my favorite girl, no matter life's confines.

To: My Aunt Dawn, who wanted to read some "happy poems."

To: My Sweetheart, who inspired too many of the poems to count. You are going to kill my rep.

Xtina Marie

Foreword

Xtina Marie's *Light Musings* has always been a side of Xtina I've seen as a fellow Nu Romantic. She may be known as the "Dark Poet Princess" in her literary circles, but she wouldn't be so good at the darkness if she didn't have equal light. She knows how to balance it in her words through the images she is known for. And it's *romantic* personified.

The Nu Romantics, a movement I started back in March of 2017, highlights the very fact that romantic and romance are different. The light and darkness we all have within ourselves and showcase in our writing is romantic. Perhaps we Nu Romantics have loosely taken the word *romantic* to separate it from the "happy ending" trope of romance and to say that romantic refers to the aesthetic beauty we find in words. Words that make us sigh. Words that mean something. Words that make us feel. That is *Nu Romanticism*. And *that* is Xtina's work.

Her poetry is a profound look at both the light and dark shades that make up our world, that give our worlds shades of color, shades that give our lives meaning and character. For what is a painting or a drawing without color and shading? It would be very one-dimensional. And that is not what makes life interesting. That is not why we love art. We want dimension. We look at all art that way, and writing is no different. It must have layers or there is no reason to read it again. And good poetry MUST be read more than once. If it needn't be, it isn't worthwhile. It doesn't cut us to our core. Xtina cuts us to our core.

"The Perfect Poem Composed," for instance, showcases Xtina's gift of light and dark through her graceful use of imagery. From sun to morning to flowers and rain, Xtina paints vivid images of beauty in very few words. Just brimming underneath is this darkness we all feel and have, and Xtina demonstrates the balance, in not only her writing in general, but within individual poems themselves. Take "You" for instance:

I'm in pain without you

my heart refusing to beat

I rip it from my chest

just to lay it at your feet

It's visceral. We feel it. That part of our bodies, the heart, so very much a symbol of love and tenderness is flipped upside down for us as we shake our heads up and down in agreement. We marvel that she can take such a cliched idea: "You're ripping my heart out" and do something fresh and alive and dark, even as it's romantic. We say to ourselves: *Damn. That would hurt.* Though we know she's using hyperbole and metaphor, not literal ideas, the pain is so visceral that we can *actually* see a hunched-over shell of a person, now dead without love. This kind of love is dangerous. And we *feel* it, like being on the edge of some riotous river that we would gladly get washed away in without the love that keeps us afloat. It's the kind of love we all dream of having. The kind of love we all search for. And the kind of love that we know will kill us, and we don't care. Because without it. We might as well be dead.

It is no different in my own poetry. My words, published in *Ruin My Lipstick*, are the same. They come from a visceral place of both light and dark. As my book says: "Poetry is what my soul bleeds when I'm not looking…" and Xtina's work is very much the same. What's strikingly different between her work and mine is that hers always (or at least almost always) rhymes. I have not been much of a fan of rhyming verse in contemporary poetry. But Xtina has changed that. Where I see other emerging poets sacrificing rhyme over content, Xtina doesn't. As a professor of English, I teach poetry for a living, and she harkens back to some of the greats, William Blake coming to mind:

I was angry with my friend;

I told my wrath, my wrath did end.

I was angry with my foe:

I told it not, my wrath did grow.

And I waterd it in fears,

Night & morning with my tears:

And I sunned it with smiles,

And with soft deceitful wiles.

And it grew both day and night.

Till it bore an apple bright.

And my foe beheld it shine,

And he knew that it was mine.

And into my garden stole,

When the night had veild the pole;

In the morning glad I see;

My foe outstretched beneath the tree.

~William Blake, The Poison Tree

She does that sort of play on words herself, one of my favorite poems of hers, published in *Pieces of Us*, The Nu Romantics' anthology, does just that, alludes to literature, like Blake does with the bible. She writes:

'How much do I love thee?'

Elizabeth said, 'Let me count the ways'

But if I tried her method

I'm afraid we'd be here for days

Xtina takes ordinary ideas and brings them to us through historical or literary eyes, creating new meaning, again, making us think and see things that weren't there the first time we read it. That. *That* is what "good" poetry is!

And Xtina isn't afraid to show the beauty of eroticism, not crude but instead, glorious. In "Love You Like Mad," she showcases the frenzied passion of love and lust, a heady aphrodisiac:

More whispered words

more loving sighs

more of this insanely

wonderful high

Or, in "Our Love," Xtina writes:

...my mind is madness

She shows the sensuality of losing oneself in passion, that "high," that loss of control and hence, the pun "mad," as we soar to a state of madness, a place where our common sense is eroded to only feeling, where all we hear behind the rushing blood behind our ears is love. That all we do is *feel*. That, dear readers, is poetry.

And that is yet another thing *Nu Romanticism* tries to address, that eroticism and sensuality are not four-letter words, but that when wrapped in love and beauty, it is part of the same gift. To ignore that our corporeal and spiritual beings are interconnected, to say eroticism is vulgar or smutty or whatever other words of disparagement have been thrown at it, ignores the human existence as fully living beings in all our facets, flawed or otherwise. We want to feel all parts of our beings: the intellectual, the emotional, the romantic, and the sensual. And when really done right, we can have them all at the same time. Xtina lets us.

Xtina Marie is a poet of our times, one that we need to pay attention to. Within the pages of *Light Musings*, every part of your being will become involved. And yes, you will read these pages again and again. They might, indeed, even sing to your Nu Romantic soul.

R.B. O'Brien, Romance Writer and Founder of The Nu Romantics

Romance Series: *Thorne, Imogen*, and *Natalie's Edge*

Poetry Collections: *Ruin My Lipstick* and *Pieces of Us*

Light Musings

A Poetic Narrative

The Perfect Poem Composed

I want to be the sun
that shines through every cloud
the familiar face
in every crowd

I want to be the rains
that cleanse you anew
the moisture on the flowers
from the morning dew

I want to be the star
that lights up the sky
that feeling you get
from a natural high

I want to be the whisper
from a gentle breeze
the rustling of the leaves
from the nearby trees

I want to be the fragrance
from the blooming flowers

the magic that you feel
in the early morning hours

I want to be the voice in your ear
when you can't hear any sound
the arms you feel
the warmth that surrounds

I want to be your sight
when your eyes are closed
the words on the page
the perfect poem composed

I want to be the touch on your skin
that eases every pain
the sparking bubbles
from the first sip of champagne

I want to be the rushing blood
and the pounding of your heart
the lighting of the match
the spark in the dark

I want to be the air in your lungs
when you've forgotten how to breathe
everything you'll ever want

everything you'll ever need

You

I'm suffocating without you
you're the air that I breathe
all of my wants, my wishes
you're everything I need

I'm blind without you
you are my vision
all that I see
my drug, my addiction

I'm deaf without you
you are my sound
your voice in my head
is the only thing around

I'm numb without you
you're my sensation
no one else could do
such a poor imitation

I'm lonesome without you
in a room full of people
in the haystack of the world
you are the needle

I'm lost without you
you give me direction
take me to class
and teach me a lesson

I'm paralyzed without you
you take away my fears
soothe all my aches
dry all the tears

I'm aching without you
you're all that I crave
I'd drop to my knees
to become your willing slave

I'm in pain without you
my heart refusing to beat
I rip it from my chest
just to lay it at your feet

I'm dying without you
I need your air to breathe
promise me, swear to me
you'll never ever leave

Your Voice

In the middle of the night
there is only your voice
I reach for myself
because I have no choice

Under your control
putty I become
you never stop
until I am done

Your whispers float softly
to my ear
I clutch the phone intently
your every word to hear

I start to react
and call your name
this ache down deep
is close to pain

The first wave is filled
with lust and heat
I ride it out
and clutch the sheet

Breathing heavy
I gasp and come down
your voice deepens as
you start the next round

I let out a giggle
tell you one will do
but I can tell by your voice
you're far from through

You're my weakness
and I start to melt
pleasure like this
I've never felt

Wave after wave
I rise and fall
hours pass
and you give me your all

I lie there complete
not a movement I make
whatever you give
I'm willing to take

Xtina Marie

Your voice becomes hoarse
it's getting late
but you tell me one more
and I can hardly wait

I've Been Thinking

Absence makes the heart grow fonder
and I believe this is true
in the silence I find
I really miss you

I kinda hate it
and love it all the same
'cause it's in the quiet that
my soul screams your name

I didn't see this coming
really did not
these feelings for you
I have really fought

But try as I might
I can't stop thinking
about you
it's the air that I'm breathing

You're just there
a constant reminder
my feelings climbing
higher and higher

I'm still trying
to put a leash on this
but I can't help wondering
how you'd kiss

How I'd fit in your arms
your scent on my skin
and I so badly want you
to let me in

I wonder if you feel
at all like I do?
Just give me a sign
just one little clue

I hate this guessing game
that I now feel
and I hate thinking
this is not really real

We don't have to say
that word that we fear
but please for my sanity
tell me you're with, my dear

Your Perfect Mistake

I think I'll become
your perfect mistake
because I know what you give
I will take

But I promise you
I mean no harm
that's what I say
while I ply you with charm

Possible warning
in the words that I say
so if you plan on leaving
I'd do it today

But please don't go
I'm quite the mess
I'll be your prefect mistake
I must confess

Worth all the smiles
and every tear
but I won't hurt you nearly
as bad as I fear

'Cause she's already done that
this I know
so you can hang on to your heart
if you need to go

And I won't blame you
not one little bit
what's left of our hearts
can't take one more hit

But I still think
we can possibly heal
help each other to awaken
and begin to feel

I'll try not to bite
unless you ask nice
I'm not sure yet
if there'll be a price

So hand me your heart
that I'd never break
and I'll still be
your perfect mistake

Never Call This Love

I've never wanted anything
quite so much
I hear your voice in my head
I dream of your touch

You consume my thoughts
and awake my senses
I've let down my guard since
you've stolen my defenses

Tore them to shreds
in such a short time
and now I'll do anything
to make you mine

Not sure if you know
exactly how I feel
but I can't quite recall
anything ever so real

You drive me insane
with what you do to my body
I want to be your good girl
even when we get naughty

My nipples harden
and my thighs get sticky
from so far away
you'd think that'd be tricky

But you've awakened me
my heart, my soul
and I'm sorry to say
that I've quite lost control

I want to take you with me
Sweetheart, my lover, my dear
I promise not to hurt you
so please never fear

Because this is frightening
for me as well
and if it were all to end now
it would hurt like hell

So let's live in the moment
feel our hearts rush with blood
forget that you said
we'd never call this love

Our Someday

I crave to put words to my thoughts
the insanity in my brain
but I don't know how
I try and try, every attempt in vain

Because there are no words
to express how I feel
and this terrifies me because
this has become so real

Tell me you love me again
it was like music to my ears
I don't care that it makes no sense
it was beautiful to hear

Because I love you, I do
with every fiber of my soul
and then I hear you tell me
that I have to learn control

I have none when it comes to you
I'm sorry to say
and since you walked into my life
I want to beg you to stay

Please don't leave
I want to beg at your feet
I know it sounds crazy
but you make me complete

Like I've been searching all my life
for what I now have found
and through time and space
by you, my heart's bound

You own my thoughts and feelings
you own my heart
and when we're not together
my soul craves you, sweetheart

I feel every path I've taken
has led me to you and you alone
and now when you are hurting
I swear I hear your moan

So don't tell me this is impossible
where there's a will, there's a way
and every second that passes
I'm working on our someday

Every

Every song on the radio
they play for you and I
every lyric, every chord
every whisper, every sigh

Every ray of sunshine
shines for me and you
every star in the sky
the many and the few

Every poem, every stanza
every last word
are about two lovers
never before understood

Every thought, every look
every caress, every kiss
is about you and I
about the now, about the this

Every time the wind blows
every time the skies rain
every time the thunder rolls
and the lightning screams your name

Every shiver of my skin
every beating of my heart
every time that we're together
every time that we're apart

Every movie romance
every storybook love
every single thing
constantly reminds me of

Every twinkle in your eye
every hair on your head
every decision I made
every place you lead

Every word that I type
every line I compose
for all the times I doubt
I know it was me you chose

For every man there's a woman
and every woman a man
and I believe with all my heart
you and I were God's plan

These Tangled Sheets

We're lying naked
in these tangled sheets
your breathing's labored
as you feel my heat

My hair is tousled
our clothes on the floor
I reach for you again
I always want more

The gleam in your eyes
says you're not done yet
I purr softly
as we start to pet

You're always ready
even when we're done
you play the game
like you've already won

You find my warmth
and you start to play
I spread for you
and let you have your way

Sticky still
from just moments before
we like it dirty
and you call me your whore

As the wave starts
I call out your name
with all this pleasure
comes a touch of pain

Still lying naked
in these tangled sheets
my body's singing
and the song is sweet

You rise above me
and my lips, you kiss
I can't believe your touch
I already miss

This crazy need we share
there is no end
my legs around you and
here we go again

Love You Like Mad

I sit here to write
to tell a quick tale
but really all I can do
is miss you like hell

To shock is my thing
to arouse or entertain
so it's not easy for me
to show you my pain

And it's painful without you
really quite so
not to make you feel bad
but I want you to know

That you've consumed me, my love
my heart and my soul
and now it's quite apparent
that I've lost all control

But you brought me to life
awakened me
and now when you're absent
I can't seem to see

It's like my eyes have gone blind
my senses stagnant
and everything else
is merely but fragments

And I find I want more
more of your time
more of your body
more of your mind

More whispered words
more loving sighs
more of this insanely
wonderful high

I want it all
and I will never want less
I always want to be
your beautiful mess

What I'm trying to say
but failing quite bad
is that I love you, my sweet
love you like mad

Where I Want to Call Home

You can call me love
bitch or baby
underneath all that
I'm still your lady

I like our little games
where I try to tell you no
even as I turn away
I do it rather slow

I want you to catch me
I want you to chase
it gives me a happy
and makes my heart race

While I like to be your whore
I also like it sweet
I like everything we do
you make me complete

Tell me that you love me
and mean it with your soul
because with you I have lost
every bit of my control

You are becoming my habit
my drug of choice
and I desperately crave
the sweet sound of your voice

So when I tell you I want more
I'm not sure what I mean
but I wanted you to know
you've become what I need

So give me the rest of you
I want to see it all
because it's too late for me
I've taken that fall

My thoughts seem all a jumble
you make my head spin
but I really think together
we can make a great win

I want your arms around me
to have you all alone
because you are fast becoming
where I want to call home

Fight

You fight what you feel
you've told me this
but I still can't stop wanting
the taste of your kiss

This will hurt like hell
when you bid me goodbye
so I can't help wondering
why it is that I try

What happens when the part of you
that fights this wins?
After I've had your love
and felt your breath on my skin?

Sometimes I wonder
just what it is you're after
and I know that without you
my heart would just shatter

I love you like mad
and I want you to stay
but I'm scared as hell
you'll soon walk away

I fight back the tears
that threaten to fall
and I wonder why I give you
every bit of my all

I don't understand why
you fight what you feel
my love, I can tell you
it is very real

So your indecision, it scares me
shakes me right to the core
because from you
all I ever really wanted was more

I hate the questions
that I am too scared to voice
but I know for me
loving you's no longer a choice

So please stop fighting
what you know in your heart
you are all that I want
all I need, sweetheart

Aching for You

Aching to hold him
to feel his arms
I've succumbed to love's touch
all of its charms

His face before me
is all that I see
distracting as hell
but a distraction I need

I dream of his touch
the soft glide of his hand
and I want to know every inch
every inch of this man

To feel as our bodies
become one in the night
knowing that this is something
so very right

Feel him slide deep
deep into my core
cling to him forever
because I'd always want more

Hear him whisper sweet words
and call out my name
to claw at his back
love drives me insane

Arch into him
as the passion builds
and wait for the sweet moment
he starts to fill

Soaked with sweat
but still wanting it all
to grab at his hair
his name I would call

Kissing his lips
never wanting to cease
I'd pull him closer
his every need, I would please

I want this only
and with all of my soul
I'm aching for you, love
I've lost all control

All That I Need

You are the beating of my heart
the blood rushing through my veins
all of my fantasies
my first kiss in the rain

You are the sparkle
that lights up my eyes
the name you hear
when my soul cries

You are my warmth
on a cold winter's night
all of my senses
my hearing, my sight

You are my sunshine
when the clouds are dark
the light that peaks through
when the rains part

You are the flowers
that bloom in their season
all of my rhymes
all of my reasons

You are stars
that worship the moon
every feeling that makes
my heart swoon

You are the swaying of the grass
that blows with the breeze
the whisper in my voice
when I tell you please

You are the lightning strikes
and the booming thunder
the magic I feel
and the spell I am under

You are my body, my mind
my soul and my heart
they have all been yours
right from the start

You are my breath
when I've forgotten how to breathe
you are everything
you are all that I need

Our Love

Our love is crazy
and all around me sparks the magic
my mind is madness
since you've wreaked all this havoc

Our love is scary
but you've chased away the fears
slayed the dragons
and made the monsters disappear

Our love is new
exciting and chaotic
my brain is fuzzy
and you leave me hypnotic

Our love is old
I've known you before
I'm completed only when you
walk through my door

Our love is rare
like a precious jewel
you're my engine
and your push, my fuel

Our love is blind
and my eyes have clouded over
but that's alright
I've taken you with me, lover

Our love is real
concrete, tangible
but still a mystery
magical

Our love is intense
consuming and insane
but without you, my love
I'm in so much pain

Our love is insatiable
I can never get my fill
I'm addicted to you
and your love my pill

Our love is forever
beyond death
I'll think of you only
as I take my last breath

Always Be the One

I wish you could see
inside my heart
I have been yours
right from the start

Your voice in my head
echoes in the quiet
I listen intently
ever so silent

I wonder what you're doing
are you thinking of me?
You've captivated my thoughts
so completely

I long for our someday
to feel your arms hold me close
and know you'll always be
the one I love most

To whisper sweet words
placing a kiss on your lips
you're my drug of choice
your love, my fix

Xtina Marie

Touching you whenever
the mood arose
telling you I love you so
you'd always know

To be the friend you tell all
your thoughts and dreams
soothing you in the night when
things don't work as they seem

I want to be there
through the ups and downs
be the one turning
your face from a frown

To be your best cheerleader
always on your side
the one you tell your secrets to
and always confide.

Sometimes love lasts
I'll prove this, my dear
when we are old
and months turn to years

Forever is Now

I'll whisper sweet nothings
into your ear
tell you I love you
year after year

I'll listen to your stories
again and again
be your lover, your confidant
and your friend

I promise to love you
in sickness and health
I promise to give you
all of myself

It's only you
to have and to hold
and it's you I'll still desire
when we are old

I want to lay in your arms
look into your eyes
I love you madly
I've come to realize

You own my heart
you own my soul
side by side
we are whole

Forever, I'll cherish you
this I vow
forever and always
and forever is now

I dream of kissing you
your lips so soft
your eyes are the one place
I want to get lost

I take your hand
fit my body to yours
forgetting everything as passion
takes its course

Because all else pales
when you are near
I'll love you forever
and forever is here

Stay

If I got down on my knees
and begged you to stay
would it change your mind?
What would you say?

Would you wrap me in your arms
whispering words I want to hear?
Would you erase my doubts
put to bed my fears?

I don't know your life's story
I just know what I feel
and believe me, love
it is quite real

I bleed with these words
my heart yours to keep
and I beg you not to hurt me
my scars have run deep

And what I want is simple
just for you to stay
for you to see inside my heart
the thoughts that it conveys

So when things get intense
and you're looking for the door
don't forget you've left me down here
helpless on the floor

You've turned my world around
there's no wrong or right
just promise to take care of me
keep me safe at night

Because I love you, baby
you mean so much to me
just love me back, I swear to you
that is my only plea

Forget all the others
that have come before
they pale in comparison since you've
walked through my door

My thoughts are jumbled
I've no words left to say
the point to all this nonsense
is I just want you to stay

Hot in the Shade

Starting to sweat
'cause it's hot in the shade
I want you so bad
yeah, I'm needing you, babe

Flesh and blood
your heart and your soul
gonna lose it all
we're outta control

Gimme a kiss
I bite at your lip
my temperature rises
when you grab my hips

It's getting so hot
sweat starts to run
I close my eyes
from the killer sun

Put your hands all over
my burning skin
my moan starts to build
from deep within

Xtina Marie

My thirst for you
cannot be sated
seems like forever
for you I've waited

I lick at the sweat that
runs down your chest
when we're done with this round
we'll have to rest

My heart's pounding
and I want to release
but I wait for you
and beg of you, please

Wrap my legs around you
as tight as can be
cling to you tightly
as we settle this need

I'm burning for you
for this love we made
wiping the sweat from my brow
'cause it's hot in the shade

No Matter Life's Confines
For Jen

Sunshine in her eyes
I know this one-of-a-kind girl
if given a chance she'd take on
the whole damn world

She's funny and sweet
sometimes a pain in my ass
but she's also the most loyal
would do anything I asked

She's always there when I need to
bitch or shoot the shit
and she never really complains
not even one little bit

She's the best one could ask for
a friend like no other
so much closer to me
than a sister or brother

I hope when she reads this
her lips part in a smile
knowing that she's been with me

for so many many miles

And though our distance limits
the fun we could be having
the hours we spend talking are
memories we're still adding

I hope she really knows
how much she means to me
and deep in her heart
I'd hope that she'd agree

We hit it off from the beginning
from the very start
and there's no way this girl
will ever leave my heart

So many crazy stories
we've had so much fun
do you remember the ghost bird, Jen?
I can't be the only one

What I'm trying hard to say
but words fail me at times
our friendship will last forever
no matter life's confines

Gypsy Woman

Gypsy woman...
she floats through this world
watch her dance...
watch her skirts when she twirls

She's the one
in your heart and your dreams
drifting by
let's crown her your queen

You try to grasp
but she's out of your reach
you want her bad
like a forbidden peach

She's on your mind
you can think of nothing more
she drives you mad
frustration to your core

She dances by
not a care in this world
so elusive
this pretty gypsy girl

What to do?
Now that she's captured your soul
you got it bad
obsession's out of control

You cry alone
no one understands
she's the one— you wish
she'd come take your hand

But she wants to fly
spread her wings and soar
you'll never catch her
as the rain begins to pour

She's like a bird
flying higher and higher
so bright
like the early morning fire

You'll never get her
give up your chase
this gypsy woman
covered in lace

The Other Shoe

The other shoe just dropped
landed with a bang
and I know right now
things will never be the same

You said you'd never hurt me
and I believe you didn't lie
but tell that to my heart
as I start to cry

I brush the tears away
I never show the pain
but I opened up to you
now you share the blame

I don't know what happened
I couldn't tell
it was around the time
I told you I fell

But pain has never been
a stranger to me
it's always good to know
who's the enemy

So I will embrace
the hurt that I feel
sometimes it's the only thing
making me real

And don't worry about me
I smile through the tears
the time that you gave
took away some fears

The other shoe—
I heard it when it dropped
and I remember you told me
that it would not

So here I am again
left alone once more
you're slowly making
your way to the door

Be gentle when you close it
please for my sake
my heart is brittle, still fractured
from the last break

Still at Your Mercy

Insanity
is my only sane
I go walking the streets
in the pouring rain

But it's sunny right now
not a cloud in sight— in fact
I believe a star, I see
in the blackest of night

I fight my straight jacket
but there is no use
the straps are too tight
I'm not getting loose

But still I try
until my arms give out
so I scream and I scream
to be let out

Suffocating in the cell
where you left me
wanting with everything
to be set free

You hold the key
that fits every lock
you are the chiming
from every clock

But you just stand there
refusing to assist
my mind breaks a little
starting to twist

My wrists are chafed
from the ropes that do bind
and the darkness closes in shattering
what's left of my mind

Was this always your plan?
I sometimes wonder
the clouds roll in
I can hear thunder

I'm still bound
still at your mercy
all I really want is
for you to save me

Sailed is this Ship

What more can I say?
What more can I do?
Nothing
so I'm through

That's it
game over
gotta straighten up
get sober

Gotta know
this is the end
say goodbye
to my best friend

I don't wanna
but it's for the best
I gave what I could
I need a rest

I gotta move on
get a grip
realize
sailed is this ship

What we had
is long gone
we're just dragging
on and on

It's not good to carry on
like this
imagining your touch
imagining your kiss

Because it just hurts
when you're not here
all over again
you disappear

All over
I feel the pain
I long to cry out
your name

So I wash my hands
set you free
wonder if
you ever loved me

Without You, My Sweet

How can I see
when my eyes have gone blind?
How can I think
when I've lost my mind?

How can I breathe
when you were my air?
How can I feel
when there's no one there?

How can I dream
when I can't close my eyes?
How can I sleep
without you by my side?

How can I live
without you in my life?
How can I die
if you have the knife?

How can I bleed
if my heart won't beat?
How do I go on
without you, my sweet?

How can I love
when you've stolen my heart?
How can I be whole
if we're apart?

How can I recover
when I can't find a cure?
How can you not know
when I'm so sure?

How can you say no
when the answer is yes?
Even though I've done wrong
and made such a mess

How can you keep walking
when I'm begging you stay?
On my knees, clutching my chest
take my pain away

Because without you, my heart
it refuses to beat
I am nothing without you
without you, my sweet

As My Heart Explodes

You left me standing
on the side of the road
I start to walk
as my heart explodes

My eyes well up
as I head toward home
but I've nowhere to go
and I'm so alone

From the heat the sweat
beads on my brow
and I've got to find a way
to go on somehow

So I keep walking
mile after mile
there's no way to make
my lips form a smile

Because I can't see
through the tears in my eyes
and my voice has grown hoarse
from all of my cries

The road is deserted
no cars in sight
it's getting dark now
day turning to night

I just keep walking
down the road all alone
time's lost all meaning
and I haven't a home

I can't stop crying
I'm stumbling around
there's nothing left
and I fall to the ground

I try to keep crawling
but I don't know to where
and I'm still sobbing
at the pain I can't bear

I finally give up
lay down in the road
embracing the pain
as my heart explodes

This Dimension

Rhyming words
and words that rhyme
in this dimension
there is no time

No right or wrong
no left or right
no sunny day
nor starry night

It's here and now
it's always there
come with me
if you dare

It's all sins of heaven
and all saints in hell
it opens up a doorway
but to where I'll never tell

It opens up my eyes
but never leaves the key
it awakens from the centuries
to set the demons free

It slowly ebbs away
and the cobwebs start to clear
and you wonder who that was
whispering in your ear

So now you've let it out
even given it a name
and your lovely life
will never be the same

It was fine while it lasted
you'll say 'til you are blue
but I really really wonder
how much of that is true

But now it doesn't matter
not a bit and not at all
and you can't exactly remember
when you took that fatal fall

You're lying in a haze
what you call "comfortably numb"
pretending not to care
for what your life's become

You Were My Air

Lying in an empty tub
the numb embraces
I settle in
while the drug chases

My eyes start to fade
tunnel vision
and I begin to think
this was a bad decision

Kinda too late now
I have to ride the ride
I don't even panic
just grip the side

But something is wrong
and I reach for you
you're with me right now
through and through

Convulsions start
but I barely feel
I can't tell if this
is really real

You are the voice of reason
I hold on to your word
chaos blooms
because everything's blurred

Getting scared now
and I need you like crazy
everything around me is
becoming so hazy

You'll keep me safe
I can give in to darkness
know that eventually
I'll come out of the nothingness

You're here with me
I'll never forget
I will forever be
in your deepest debt

When I grasped for you
you were right there
I was drowning in the tub
and you were my air

The Heart

The heart is deceitful
the good book tells
was it lying when it told me
in love with you, I fell?

I fell hard and fast
it didn't take long
my heart doesn't care
what is right or wrong

The heart is wicked
it teaches us to sin
but with you I was already
willing to give in

I wanted you so bad
from the moment that we met
I couldn't wait for you to make
me your little pet

The heart is black
like an abyss
but I'd close my eyes
when we'd start to kiss

The whole world stops
when you whisper 'I love you'
even though the heart lies
I believe that it is true

The heart is not a friend
only a foe
perhaps that's why
I can't let you go

Because I've tried, I have
to set you free
but then you whisper in my ear
that you love me

The heart is bloody
and bleeds out fast
is that why it's so hard
to make love last?

Because you said you loved me
and I believed it was true
that's the reason I let myself
fall in love with you

I Was Your Fool

Patterns
I'm just one that you repeated
before it had begun
I was defeated

Hurt me
you did, was that your plan?
I'm trying hard
to understand

I really loved you
that's what stings
when you know the truth
give it a ring

Was I a prize
the goal or the game?
I guess it doesn't matter
the result is the same

I was your fool
and you played me well
what happens next?
Only time will tell

Forgetting you won't be easy
you've touched my soul
that's why it wasn't hard
to lose control

Hate you
never, it's not my style
but I haven't been hurt like this
in a long while

You taught me well
with all of your lies
for my own peace of mind
I'm cutting the ties

So before you spin
another one of your tales
know it's your own cross
and you've got the nails

You've done this to you
you are to blame
watch all that you've loved
go up in flames

Behind These Words of Mine

My muse sings to me softly
whispers in my ear
if you listen closely
his words become clear

He tells me little secrets
about life and love
I could listen for hours
and never get enough

He visits while I'm dreaming
comes to me at night
holds my hand in darkness
tells me everything's all right

He is the inspiration
behind these words of mine
the answer to the riddle
the flow to every rhyme

In my head I hear his voice
it colors all I do and say
I don't even think he knows
how much pain he's took away

So when I'm deep in thought
my muse is on my mind
he's never far away
no matter the day or time

Still I wait and wonder
for inspiration to impart
he'll speak it rather softly
but always to my heart

Then my words burst out faster
faster than before
I can't even try to hide them
they're not easy to ignore

No one has spoke so strongly
to my very soul
I let the words surround me
it's out of my control

He whispers to me now
what it means I can't confuse
it's the truth he always tells me
even though he's just my muse...

Xtina Marie

I've Been Thinking About You

I've been thinking about you
do you think about me too?
Your voice in the night
makes everything all right

I've been dreaming about you
will my dreams come true?
Change— some things never will
it's my heart that suffers still

I've been reminded of a time
when you were just mine
nothing else really mattered
that's when everything shattered

Now I'm left with this hole
it reaches straight to my soul
nothing can replace
that look of love on your face

But I'll keep trying, I'm sure
to find a love that's so pure
because without you it's cold
and there's nothing to hold

I'll think back to that day
when you went away
I'll look at your picture in a frame
and know that I was to blame

And I'll always wonder why
I decided to lie
why I couldn't be myself
and trust you'd want nothing else

So I'll still think about you
will you think about me too?
Call me in the night
I'll make everything all right

You'll be the hero in my dreams
killing the bad things
I'll never want to wake
it's all for love's sake

Remember the time
when you were just mine?
I love you still
I always will

Xtina Marie

My Heart is Beating Still

You warm my heart
and make me whole
I want to hang on tight
and not let go

Just a thought
and I start to heat
my cold heart stirs
and starts to beat

It's been so long
years and years
but you slay the dragons
and free the fears

Make me laugh
and come alive
you kick my soul
into overdrive

Are you a phantom
some kind of dream?
On the inside
I start to scream

Where once was nothing
now a spark
because deep inside
you've released the dark

Reminded me
nothing's set in stone
I can do what I want
make it my own

I feel beautiful
and worth the while
I think of you and
can't hide the smile

You've taught me how
to embrace the rain
that life is more
than tears and pain

It's what you make it
make it what you will
I have to go on living
because my heart is beating still

Xtina Marie

This I Solemnly Swear

I promise to look for you
in the next life
amid all the struggles
and all of the strife

I'll whisper your name
as I die my death
in hopes that it's the first thing
I breathe with my breath

Wherever you are
you'll beckon my soul
because it's never 'til I find you
that I become whole

Maybe we'll meet
on a mountain somewhere
but find you I will
this I solemnly swear

Maybe I'll be walking
in the pouring rain
and the lightning that strikes
will scream out your name

And maybe sight-seeing
near the Rio Grande
or it could just be a beach
with my feet in the sand

To the ends of the earth
I swear I will look
and I won't even care
how much time that it took

In this life that we met
it wasn't our time
but I promise in the next
you will be mine

So with my last breath
your name will I breathe
you'll be in my soul
as this world I do leave

I won't quit looking
I do now confess
for the search is bound
to be a success

Some Writing on the Wall

Wiggling my toes
because this water's gotten cool
I look for you
because you've taken me to school

I kinda hate it
but love it just the same
tell me that you feel it
this cat and mouse game?

But you won't tell me the rules
and I'm looking to play
I'm kinda getting lost
and you've taken my toys away

You say life is better as a comedy
and I can agree
but how 'bout we make the rating
spicier than PG?

You've told me the water is warm
brought me to life
made me see how fun it can be
playing with the knife

But now I'd like a little more
of what's behind the mask
and while you're really really good
I've just remembered to ask

So let me in
I'm like Toto with the curtain
peeling it back
hoping to heal your hurtin'

Because at the end of the day
all I have to do is feel
move my toes a little
to know what's really really real

And if this is all there is
some writing on the wall
that's pretty cool too
who doesn't enjoy a fall?

So I wiggle my toes
feel the warmth around me
and I'll never forget
who it was that taught me...

Some Writing on the Wall
part 2
or 'This F*cking Riddle'

A cat and mouse game
and we're both on the prowl
I'm here to tell you
that I can really growl

I think you know this
and that's why we dance
a little of the dirty
and a little romance

The more I give you
the more you seem to take
but I'll be damn sure it won't be
my heart you break

I'm not sure who's winning
but we go 'round and 'round
It may not even matter
I still give you pound for pound

What is real

and what's a game?
it's hard to tell
when you moan my name

I have to convince myself
it's just writing on the wall
but it's getting harder and harder
not to admit the fall

So when you tell me you love me
make sure that it's true
because this feeling for me
is really really new

When did this happen
and when did it start?
Seems like it's been forever
since you've stolen my heart

So, let's play some more
because I'm in the lead
I don't think I'll ever
admit defeat

It's certainly possible
that we meet in the middle

if I could just decipher
this f*cking riddle

Some Writing on the Wall
part 3
or 'This Beautiful Flame'

Maybe I should stop playing
admit defeat
because it's starting to feel
like you make me complete

I worry that it's more for me
than for you
I've just decided
to believe that it's true

The pieces of the puzzle
may not be missing
I just couldn't see them
too busy not listening

With eyes wide open
I think I've surrendered my heart
it was yours to begin with
ever since the kick start

As the words start to flow
I'm reminded I'm alive
fingers typing faster
my soul's hit overdrive

And for that, that alone
it's worth a little pain
and I know in my heart
life will never be the same

Sometimes you need toe wiggling
to recall
that the water's always been warm
after all

So no more confusion
and no more games
there's no putting out
this beautiful flame

The riddle's been solved
it took me a while
but you're worth every heart flutter
every smile

Just some writing on a wall?

I think it's safe to say
that my heart beats for you
day after day...

Slam it on Home

In the grocery store
and your hands get grabby
I want you so bad
can I call you daddy?

I push your hands away
and whisper no
and I like it that it leads
to you wantin' mo'

I sway my hips a little
and your eyes get brighter
you like it that your bad girl's
such a fighter

My handsome devil likes it
when I start to scream
slide my panties over
and let you feel my cream

Oh that's so bad
I wanna suck your d*ck
I don't think the store
is ready for this sh*t

But we can't stop touching
and I need your all
you push my back against
some unused wall

I grab at your belt
as you yank my shirt
if we don't hurry up
I know you'll have to squirt

Man, that's so gross
I just had to giggle
but that's how you like it
and I start to wiggle

I want you inside me, baby
take me now
I'm sweating so bad
can you wipe my brow

You slam it on home
and we start the show
f*ck me hard and fast
let me feel you blow

Xtina Marie

Something I Need

I must be careful
remember to breathe
you're fast becoming
something I need

You've set my body
on fire
say you don't want me
and you're a liar

I'm hot and breathless
you're all consuming
my body quivers
from what you're doing

I want you to lick me
off your fingers
on your lips I want
my taste to linger

I wrap my hand tight
around you
get you ready for
round two

I call your name and
start to tremble
this feeling's more than
I can handle

The wave washes
ever so sweetly
I lay there satisfied
and oh so completely

You dip a finger
in my wetness
offered to me
and tell me "taste this"

I suck it greedily
then lick my lips
you growl intensely
and grab my hips

I brace myself
as you slide in
I move to meet you
and we begin

A Deep Breath of You

I take a drink of you
you fill my every need
I take a deep breath of you
you're the air that I breathe

I want to hold you close
and never let you go
you're a part of me
yeah, you complete my soul

When I'm with you
all the world stands still
you're like the pharmacist
and your love— my pills

You're everything I want
you're my desire
an overwhelming lust
an all-consuming fire

Everywhere I go
your face is all I see
you've opened up my eyes
and made me believe

I take your hand and place it
directly on my heart
it was dead for so long
but you've gotten it to start

I want to love you
for the rest of my life
If this is gonna kill me
then I'd gladly take the knife

Because without you, baby
I'm cold and alone
I'm sure if you listened
you could hear my moan

I want your breath on my cheek
your hand in my hair
I take a deep breath of you
you're my source of air

I take a big drink of you
you fill my cup
I don't know how this happened
but with you, I fell in love

Devouring

You're killing me, confusing me
and twisting me around
but I'm hanging on, by a thread
feels like I'm gagged and bound

I never know, what's in your head
makes me want you even more
I'm sacrificing, giving in
and begging at your door

You will be the death of me
I feel my heartbeat slow
with every word, you don't say
silence becomes a blow

I want to hear you call my name
whispering words so sweet
you've captured me, heart and soul
and that is no easy feat

I want you now, every inch
passion's stronger every hour
I don't know what you've done

but you hold me in your power

I want to stay, within your grasp
you're never close enough
you're consuming me, devouring
with this crazy love

The need burns in, deep in my brain
you're always on my mind
one step away from dangerous
no reason or no rhyme

I think you feel the same as me
I think that's why you ran
it's too late now, I've got your scent
I think you understand

There's no hope, this love's
gonna kill and devour us alive
just give in, our fate is sealed
later on we'll cry

So take my hand lead me on
there's nothing more to do
end of story, there is no more
it's because I love you

Dirty Little Secret

I don't believe in fate
but the planets have aligned
and now it's getting hard
to keep you out of my mind

It's more than just a friendship
but I'm not yet sure a name
maybe there isn't one
but it's way more than a game

In a game there are rules
ones set in stone
but at the end of the day
we don't want to be alone

I've got your back
as you do mine
we made a promise
the pinky-swear kind

That we would always be honest
even brutally so
and I place my trust in that
I wanted you to know

I will never hurt you
always be on your side
be an open ear
when you need to confide

So just know that I am here
to give whatever you need
I'll be your friend
when your heart needs to bleed

You do something to me
it's kinda hard to admit
sometimes I think we'd really make
quite a good fit

I laugh at your jokes
and my heart cries with your pain
broken people can mend each other
when there's no one left to blame

This world can be cruel
we can both attest to this
and sometimes I'd give anything
for just one little kiss

But shhh, don't tell a soul
'cause I'm your dirty little secret
and as long as I am living
I promise you I'll keep it

The One with the Master Key

Have you ever made a mistake
but one you'd gladly do again?
I'm there right now
and I'm taking you with me, my friend

Sorry that I sucked you in
to this madness that is me
but you came so fast
and so very willingly

You're more than just a distraction
this, I really swear— and I'm
hoping that when the time comes
it's my heart you can repair

'Cause this one is gonna hurt
I walked in eyes wide open
for some reason, a happy ending
really was what I was hoping

But as luck would have it
I've been cursed in love
it's rather old news and I cry tears
soaked in my blood

That's when you showed up
made my heart smile
said I didn't have to walk alone
for so many miles

Between a rock and a hard place
I think the saying goes
but who has made it past
to watch the door close?

You say you'll stand beside me
and give me a helping hand
and I kinda wish you didn't
because without you I can't stand

So now I'm asking you
and falling to my knees
and I hate the fact
that I just begged you please

Not to forget I'm down here
and waiting patiently
and I only really wait on
the one with the master key

Xtina Marie

Screaming Out Your Name

Lying here
my body thoroughly used
I like it when by you
I feel totally abused

Breathing heavy
trying to come down
but you whisper in my ear
and I'm wet from the sound

You're killing me
and I'm just about through
but I like it when
you tell me what to do

My thighs are sticky
and I still want you more
I love that you never make
me your dirty whore

I want to make this real
you inside of me
my legs wrapped around you
never wanting to be free

I want to climb atop you
f*ck you hard and deep
make sure when we are done
me— you'd always want to keep

I want you dripping out of me
all the love you gave
and I promise that you
I'd always always crave

Do dirty things to me
grab me from behind
plunge in hard and fast
'til my eyes go blind

I want to keep you hard
hard and deep inside
I want to always f*ck you
feel our bodies as we grind

Kiss my breath away
let's light this heady flame
be sure that when we're done
I'll be screaming out your name

Your Work of Art

I've got this crush
and it's crushing me
I try to look past it
but you're all I see

First thing in the morning
last thing at night
and when the doubts creep in
you make everything all right

You've given me hope
for so long there was none
and I kinda hate that
for you, I'm not the one

When I write, it's with honesty
and I spill my soul
so it's with this that I tell you
you've become my goal

I won't give up
so you can forget that noise
I'll make loving me
your favorite choice

I'm persistent
as you already can attest
so there's no way in hell
I'll give it a rest

Mark my words
you can fight all you want
but I'm in your head
where I will haunt

It's me that you will think of
I will make you smile
because you've been with me
for some messed up miles

Not sure why it was you
but that's in the past
and I don't care what you say
I'd never ask

I'll demand a place
close to your heart
and I will always be
your work of art

Xtina Marie

Playtime

Forbidden
taboo
is that why
I want you?

Burning
desire
we're playing
with fire

On your knees
you say
and I drop
to obey

Abuse my
body
make me
naughty

You say harder
then faster
I worship
my master

You bring pleasure
then pain
what a
dangerous game

Bite
while I scratch
come light
my match

I 'm
your pet
let me lap
at your sweat

With your hands
feel me up
would you drink
from my cup?

Claw
'til I bleed
I'm yours
plant your seed

Micro Shorts

A micro short is a short, intense story told in 300 words or less. Think a Haiku and a novel have a baby.

Long Distance

"Your go." She pushes play, ending her turn, and cradles the phone between her shoulder and ear while getting comfortable in bed. It's late, creeping toward one a.m. but she never wants her nights with him to end.

"That's not a word," she hears him mutter his frustration, knowing he'll take his time and try every combination of letters he has, until he's satisfied he's found the best word.

She faces the fan to blow directly on her face, it's warm, close to hot on this long summer night. "I love you," she whispers. He doesn't respond, but she's sure he heard. She smiles, her heart warm and full of her love for him.

High on Love

"I'm getting close," I whisper to him, my voice shaky and all of my muscles starting to clench up.

"Me too," he's barely coherent, and I smile, knowing what I'm doing to him. I bite my lip as the waves wash over me, taking him with me.

We lay there in silence while we catch our breath, a thin sheen of sweat on our skin. Every nerve ending I have hums and my head- I feel almost high. I am high. I am high on him. High on love. I am addicted, and I hope I never find the cure.

8:29 Forever

"It's getting late," he said, glancing at the clock on the nightstand.

She knew he had to be to work early the next morning, knew that their weekend together had drawn to a close- again. Grabbing the cord to the clock, she gave it a tug- stilling the second hand as it was lazily making its way around the dial.

"What are you doing?" Before he could get up, she'd crawled behind him and encircled her arms around his shoulders. She kissed his neck, smelling her perfume on his skin. "You don't have to go yet, it's only 8:29."

He smiled and leaned back into her- wishing that it would remain 8:29 forever.

Everything and Nothing

'What are you doing?' It's late but I text him anyway, knowing he's still awake. 'Nothin', he replies just moments later. I pick up the phone and dial his number by heart- I know it better than I know my own number.

As soon as I hear his voice, I melt. "Hey, sweetheart," I lay back in bed, cradling my cell.

"Whatdya want?" he sounds annoyed, but I know he really isn't.

I giggle. "You." He groans and I giggle again.

"We just talked an hour ago!"

"So." He sighs, and I get comfortable, knowing we'll talk late into the night. About everything and nothing at the same time.

Broke Down on a Country Road

"Can I trouble you for some water, miss?" he asks, his voice low and gruff.

She fights not to giggle, knowing they've played out this little fantasy of hers before, but it never gets old. She bites her lip and reaches in through the open window of her car to grab a bottle of water before holding it out to him.

He takes it from her, his hand lingering a moment or two. He nods his head in the direction of the road. "The bike broke down a few miles back."

She looks up at him, smoothing her yellow sundress down her shapely legs, feigning innocence and lets out a yelp of surprise when he lifts her off her feet and slams her down onto his leather jacket that covers the trunk of the car. "Please, don't hurt me," she whispers, still fighting not to grin.

When he wrestles himself between her legs and crushes his mouth to hers, she lets out a groan and wraps her legs around his waist.

Exhilarating

The little girl came to a jolting stop by bearing down hard on the rubber-heel brake at the back of her skate. She swiped a hand over her forehead, absentmindedly pushing dark strands of messy bangs out of her eyes. Her heart beat crazily in her chest and her legs felt like she had electricity running through them.

Exhilarating. She thought that might be the word she was looking for. Exhilarating. She wasn't positive, mind you. She was only nine, and while she read a lot, she by no means knew all the words yet.

Before she could even fully catch her breath, she pushed off, and headed toward the little hill where she would make the climb to the top just so that she could skate down the other side at break-neck speed, hoping a car was not coming. It had never happened yet. *Yet*, being the key word.

For those brief moments, as she raced to the bottom, she felt like she was flying. For right now- all of her nine years- it was the best feeling in the world.

He Doesn't Say It Back

"I love you," I whisper to him and he chuckles but doesn't say it back.

"You always love me after sex."

I smile, leaning closer to plant a kiss on his still warm lips. "True. But, I love you all the time."

I sigh and go to move- extracting myself from his arms. Before I have made it, he's tightening his grip on my messy ponytail and hauling me back in place. He flexes, and I'm surprised to feel him still hard beneath me. My breath catches as I sink back down and around him, our eyes locking. Still, he doesn't tell me he loves me. And that's okay- his words do not need to. His eyes tell me all the time.

Christmas With You

We sat beside the Christmas tree on some blankets you'd thrown down, the fireplace warming our skin, '*Merry Christmas, Baby'* playing softly in the background. The lights from the tree cast multiple colors over your face as you hand me a wrapped gift. A spark of electricity shoots through my fingers as our hands touch. I bite my lip when my tummy tightens, anticipation coursing through me. I tear open the paper with no finesse, anxious to find out what you've picked out for me. "*The Kama Sutra*?" I ask, staring at the cover, gliding my hand over its glossy front. "And.." my voice trails off. "You wanted to demonstrate it with me?" I can feel the heat climbing up my neck to redden my face some.

"God, no," you chuckle. "There are some crazy positions in there that would kill us." Your eyes twinkle. "What did you get me?"

I hand you over the wrapped present I have behind me. You are quiet while you open it, a far deal more eloquent at it than I had been.

You see it is a first edition of your favorite book. You smile. "I am touched," you tell me as you lean in to cover my lips with your own. You kiss me softly, your tongue running over the seam of my mouth until I part my lips. A small moan climbs up my throat and my heartbeat quickens.

It's just minutes after Christmas, and if I don't get another thing, it will still be the very best Christmas of my entire life. Under the tree, in the warmth of your arms, your lips moving softly over mine. You are the best present I could ever have wished for.

What He Gave Her

"-And he got me this beautiful bracelet!" Andrea lifted her bony wrist in the air, displaying the charms, her smile pulling her lips up and sharpening her cheekbones.

The other office girls ooohed and aaahed, Kristen included. They all took turns bragging on what wonderful gifts their boyfriends had bestowed upon them for Christmas.

Andrea turned to Kristen. Looked at her expectantly. "What did Evan get you?"

Kristen's eyes lowered a bit. "We didn't do gifts this year." She turned and started back to her cubicle, a smile playing across her features, remembering. Remembering his breath, warm against her ear, his strong arms around her. His voice- that beautiful, deep voice as he vowed his love, as he painted the vivid picture in her mind of the two of them holding hands, wrinkled by age.

He didn't need to spend money on an expensive bracelet. What he gave her could never be placed inside a box with a lovely red bow. Her gave her himself.

Conspiracy Theories & Aliens

"So, the point I was making," he says, and she smiles, just loving hearing him talk, not even totally sure what it is he's talking about anymore. Could be conspiracy theories, could be aliens, could be politics- none of these topics are any she'd ever choose to talk about on her own, but that doesn't much matter either.

She watches him as he talks, taking in his gorgeous brown eyes- so warm, and his dark brown hair that's beginning to silver in some places, his lips- plump and so kissable.

He pauses, distracted. "Are you even listening to me?"

She meets his eyes, "Mmmmmhmmmm," she tells him, and her heart flutters in her chest when he starts to talk again.

Conspiracy theories *and* aliens this time. She was close. Again, it doesn't matter- she could listen to him talk forever. *'The point is,'* she thinks- the smile back on her face- *'you're mine.'*

About the Author

The Accidental Poet:

Xtina Marie is an avid horror and fiction genre reader, who became a blogger; who became a published poet; who became an editor; who now is a podcaster, and an aspiring novelist—and why not? People love her words.

Her first book of poetry, Dark Musings has received outstanding reviews in addition to being nominated for a Bram Stoker Award for poetry. It is likely she was born to this calling. Writing elaborate twisted tales to entertain her classmates in middle school would later lead Xtina to use her poetry as a private emotional outlet in adult life—words she was hesitant to share publicly—but the more she shared, the more accolades her writing received.

Later in the year, Xtina's dark poetry fans will be treated to some of her darkest work ever in her third book, titled Darkest Sunlight.

Her first romance erotica novel is well under way but has taken a back seat to an ever-increasing number of commitments.

Other dark poetry titles from HellBound Books for your delectation…

Dark Musings

Dark Musings by Xtina Marie

The perfect companion piece to Light Musings – The dark side of Xtina Marie's poetry delves into intense emotions: heartache, loss, hurt, pain, rage, and a dangerous consuming love which can drive one insane. Dark Musings is not a collection!

The author returned to the centuries old practice of Narrative Poetry—the telling of a story through poetry. If you believe you are brave enough to explore the savage emotions of the human heart; Dark Musings will test your mettle.

<u>Insights into Evil Insides</u>

TRIGGER WARNING!
If easily offended or of a sensitive nature, please do not purchase.

Dark, disturbing poetry, definitely not for the faint of heart - a singularly unique delve into the core of a troubled soul...

In what is a slow descent into something much different than before, Insights to Evil Insides tells a story of how the sinister creeps and lurks behind closed doors..

It takes over more than you know, and it's more than you can control....

Obsession and control are large themes as well, Torment that is both physical and psychological. A blood Obsession is prominent. My Evil sides are predominant.

You won't understand the depth until you read and experience it.

Beautiful Tragedies

Only through dark poetry can a tragedy become something truly beautiful.

"Beauty is in the eye of the beholder." This phrase has origins dating back to ancient Greece, circa 300 BC; proving that some humans have always had the ability to see beauty where others could not.

Beautiful Tragedies is a compilation of 140 works by no less than fifty-five amazing poets writing in a variety of forms--all inspired by feelings born in the darkest of times.

They express the pain associated with unrequited or all-consuming love gone wrong, as well as where the resulting emotions can take us. Readers will get in touch with the darkness lurking inside all of us—the ugly part of us—where we can consider the unthinkable, stemming from the madness gripping our minds.

<u>Detours and Dead Ends</u>

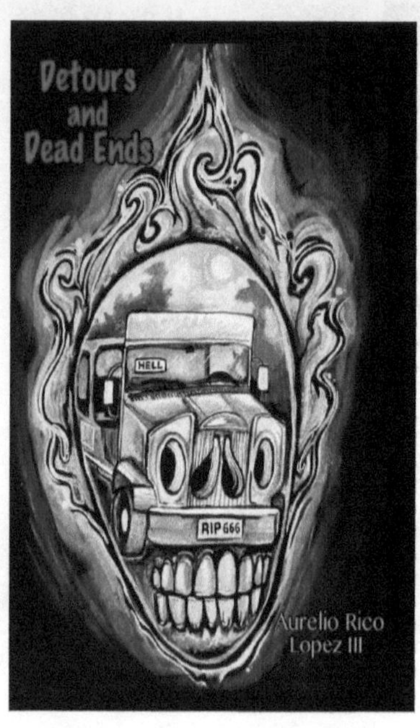

There are so many poems that invoke feelings of romance, wonderment, and joy.

These aren't them.

Aurelio Rico Lopez III is an exceedingly talented writer and poet who manages to conjure up scenes of mayhem, fear, and cosmic dread in this poetry collection, Detours and Dead Ends.

Lopez brings a bit of artistic flare to his signature style of writing and provides a book that takes the reader from murder to revenge, from unfortunate circumstances to several different flavors of the apocalypse.

So crack it open and enjoy the ride..

Tripping Balls

A thought provoking, eclectic, disturbing and at times downright weird collection of poetry, short stories and insightful musings from the inimitable Gocni Schindler....
He offers a variety of stories which beautifully gives the awesome reader, like you, the opportunity to experience different levels of thought and contemplation. I know, it's so exciting! God willing, some humor as well.

 The book takes off with a top shelf short story titled Hell-A-Expense. Super! Within this tale, the Demon takes possession of its victim and takes you along for the ride as a co-conspirator. Don't do anything I wouldn't do! Step right up, step right up! Meet Johnny B Fast and the tale of Dynamic Drunken Disorderly. Damn, that's a memory! Moving along, moving along,

Oh, yes, we stop at the tale of Henrietta and her treacherous trip. What a bitch! Insane is sexual. Oh, look, another fine telling of a good story! Mental Blues and a possible moment at the mental ward. 'Innocent I tell you, I'm innocent!' Stop right there! Let me introduce you to the Homeless man, Ronin, and that good buddy Actor Man and yes, there is an almighty telling of their rotten tales.

**A HellBound Books LLC
Publication**

www.hellboundbookspublishing.com

Printed in the United States of America

9 781948 318150